You are an Amazing Boy

A Collection of Inspiring Stories about Courage, Friendship, Inner Strength and Self-Confidence

Nadia Ross

Special Art Stories

You are an Amazing Boy

A Collection of Inspiring Stories about Courage, Friendship, Inner Strength and Self-Confidence

Nadia Ross

PAPERBACK ISBN: 979-12-80592-50-7

support@specialartbooks.com
www.specialartbooks.com

Table of Contents

Introduction | 4

Ian Goes to Camp | 7

Jack and the Rock Concert | 19

Connor Presents His Science Project | 30

Luke Makes a Movie | 41

Adam is Too Tall | 51

Elijah Builds a Tree Fort | 63

Cooper and the Chess Tournament | 73

Julian Learns Something New | 81

Dylan and the Tree Swing | 89

Sebastian and His Brother
Build a Rocket | 98

Epilogue | 108

Introduction

Hello, adventurous and amazing boy. Do you know that you are very special? You are unique, which means there is only one of you in the entire world. Do you know how incredible that is? This planet has billions of people on it, and there is no one like you on it. You have a wonderful way of looking at the world. You are brave, funny, intelligent, and incredible. It would help if you always remembered that. Only you know how to shine the special light inside you, and only you can give that light to others.

The challenges in the world will sometimes be big and sometimes be small. These challenges may scare you at times, or sometimes they may bring you doubt. But don't get down on yourself. We all have these feelings. Your parents, brothers, sisters, grandparents, friends, and even strangers all feel the same emotions you do.

But even when you are afraid, you can still work past your fear. When you are doing something new or trying some-thing hard, you may have difficulty start-ing it, but the things you fear the most will sometimes give you the best experi-ence. Plus, any mistakes you make, you learn from and find goodness in each thing you do, even when you find that things are harder than you thought they would be.

This book has a bunch of boys in it who are brave and strong like you. They go through the same things you do each day. They get scared, worried, and once in a while they don't win, but they work hard, keep trying, and learn from their mistakes until they get things right.

Even when they get discouraged or begin to doubt their abilities, they find that unique light inside themselves that helps them keep going, even when they think about giving up. Within each story, these boys find self-confidence, hope, and bravery that allows them to have an amazing experience in every situation they are in, which helps them reach their ultimate goals.

It's time to shine your light on your corner of the world. Bring it to other people, let go of fear, and learn the lessons of life. Believe in yourself, and you can accomplish anything.

You are an amazing boy!

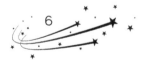

Ian Goes to Camp

Have you ever gone to a new place with new people and got to do new things? How did it feel? Did you get nervous

or get jitters in your belly before you started? Did you wonder about what the new stuff would actually be like? Did you worry about what the new people would say, do, and how they would act? Did you think about not going because you were so nervous?

Guess what? Everyone gets nervous, and you may think that it means you shouldn't do something when really it's the opposite! When you get nervous and worry about how things will turn out, it actually means you care about how things are going to go. If you are scared about making new friends, know that you, amazing boy, are fantastic, and if you are true to yourself, you'll find friends who like you for who you are.

~ ~ ~

Ian was packing his bags to get ready for summer camp. He was very excited about going. He loved fishing, camping, and doing pretty much anything out-side. He loved it so much that his mom actually signed him up for the outdoors-man camp this year. It was his first year of going to a camp like this, and while he was a bit nervous about being away from home for the first time, his mom had shown him all of the special activi-ties he would get to do.

Ian was excited to try everything. The camp had canoeing, archery, fishing, horse riding, hiking, swimming, and more.

9

He wasn't sure what he would try first. Still, ever since his mom had told him about going away for three weeks and what he was going to be able to do, he had been daydreaming about shooting a bow and arrow and hitting the target right in the center, riding a horse and jumping over barrels, and canoeing on the lake while catching the biggest fish possible.

He honestly couldn't wait.

Ian's mom brought in the mail at dinner time a few nights before he was ready to go. She opened a letter from the camp and read it to the family. "Dear Ian, please note that your bunkmates will be David, Jeremy, and Thomas. They are the same age as you are, and you will be staying in bunk number 17."

Ian flinched.

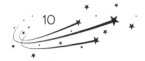

He had never spent the night with any-one before except his grandparents, brother, and parents. "What are bunk-mates?" he asked. Even though he was pretty sure they were other boys, he thought he would be staying within a tent.

"Sweetie," his mom said. "We talked about this, remember? There are four boys to a cabin, and in that cabin, you'll have four beds and four dressers, and they are the group you'll be doing ev-erything with."

"I didn't know that would mean we would be sleeping in the same room together."

Suddenly, Ian grew nervous. Not only had he never been away from home for a long time, but he had never had to meet new people without his family around. What if the boys in his cabin

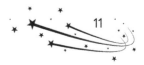

didn't like him? What if they thought his daydreaming was weird, or what if they didn't think he was good at anything?

Now Ian became really, really nervous.

Instead of saying anything else or asking any more questions, Ian started thinking of all the things that could go wrong. The fear about the bad stuff was ballooning up in his chest. He was no longer able to find any of the excitement that he originally had before his mom read him the letter.

He wondered what the other boys would be like. Would they be nice or mean? Would they like to sleep with a nightlight on? Would they try to scare him when he was sleeping? Would they do anything weird like putting a snake or mouse in his bed?

"Ian."

Ian blinked and was brought back to the dinner, where everyone was almost finished eating. He looked down at his plate and saw that he had barely eaten anything. Ian also realized that he was no longer hungry. He got up and cleared his plate off, put it in the sink, and started walking to his bedroom in a fog of concern about what would be happening when he got to camp.

"Hey, Ian!" Jonathan, Ian's brother ran up beside him and nudged his arm. "Didn't you hear me ask a question?"

Ian shook his head no, he was still a little too concerned to respond with a full answer. Even though Ian knew his shock would wear off soon, he also knew that Jonathan wouldn't think badly of him because he was not speaking yet.

"What's going on? You were quiet throughout dinner and you didn't even eat! I thought that was your favorite meal?" Ian did like hamburgers and potatoes, they were his favorites. Now that Jonathan pointed out that he hadn't eaten anything, Ian's stomach crunched a bit with hunger.

But Ian couldn't shake the worry off of his shoulders.

"I don't know. I think when Mom said that I would have to bunk with other people, people I don't even know, it made me really, really nervous."

Ian stopped walking to lean up against the wall in the hallway.

Jonathan—who was already a teenager, was quite a few years older than Ian, so he was also much taller than Ian who

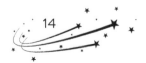

14

hadn't hit a growth spurt yet—leaned over and put his arm around his brother. "What are you nervous about?" Jonathan asked.

"A lot of things," Ian said. He had forgotten all the good things he was thinking about when he first heard about the camp, and now he was just worried about what he would have to do to NOT go. "What if the people I am staying with don't like me? What if they make fun of me? What if they put snakes in my bed or spiders in my hair while I sleep? How am I supposed to sleep with boys I've never met before? If they don't like me, how are we supposed to do all the activities together?" The more Ian thought about it, the more worried he became. . .

"Whoa!" Jonathan said. "Hold on there, little brother. Remember all the good

15

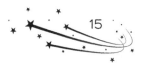

things. Plus, what happens if your bunk-mates like you?"

Ian blinked and looked at Jonathan. He hadn't thought about that. "Oh," he said as he began to remember that he did have a lot of friends at school. In fact, he really had always gotten along with everyone.

"And no matter what happens, little bro, I'll always like you and always be your friend. So you're never really going to be alone. Just like I'm never really alone too, because I always have you."

Ian smiled at that. He liked the idea that no matter what, he and Jonathan would always have each other. "That's true," Ian said. A wave of relief washed over him, and Jonathan reached out to pull him into a brotherly hug.

"Come on. Let's go get you something to eat now. I'm sure you are hungry. You didn't even touch your dinner!"

So, Ian and Jonathan got a few more things to eat so they weren't hungry for the rest of the night. The next day, Ian finished packing up. When they dropped him off at camp, Jonathan reminded him that he wasn't ever really alone.

The next three weeks for Ian were fantastic, and he had a great amount of fun. Not only did he make friends with his bunkmates, he also made friends with a lot of other people. Everyone at the camp loved doing the same things that Ian did, and they all had so much to talk about.

At night, when Ian was lying in bed, he couldn't wait to tell his brother about his amazing adventures at camp. But he

didn't want to leave camp too early because he still had so much more to do!

~ ~ ~

So, have you ever been nervous about meeting new people? Now do you know that even when you have this fear, you'll be able to have the experience and make new friends? People will like you for who you are, and no matter where you go, as long as you are yourself, you will find someone who likes what you like and does what you do.

Jack and the Rock Concert

Have you ever loved something so much you wanted to share it with your friends? Did you hope that they loved the idea

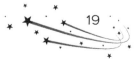

just as much as you did? Did you ever think what would happen if your friends wanted to share your vision with many more people, as an audience, and they wanted you to lead the way?

What would happen if you had to stand up with a group of people watching you do something for the first time in front of them? Do you think you would be able to do it? You can overcome anything to show the world who you are.

~ ~ ~

Jack loved listening to music. He loved music so much that he played a lot of instruments. The instrument he enjoyed playing the most was guitar. He listened to music in the morning before school, in the afternoon when he was doing his homework, and watched a lot of music videos too. Any time he had a chance to

go to a concert in the park with his parents, he would be there. On the weekends he would play his guitar and learn new songs.

One afternoon, he was watching one of his favorite bands stream live in concert and he got struck with a great idea. He realized that he should form a band too! Jack had a few friends that he knew also played musical instruments. He made a plan to talk to them to see who was interested.

The next day, Jack talked to his friends and they thought that Jack had an amazing idea! They decided to get together after school with their instruments, to see what kind of music they should play together.

Jack was so excited. He could barely pay attention the rest of the day in school.

He was very thankful for how quickly the day went. After he got home, he talked to his parents who gave permission to have his friends over after he did his homework. Jack called them to let them all know, and he finished his homework in record time.

After he was done, he went into the basement to set up an area where they could all play. They would have two guitars, one singer, one set of drums, and one keyboard. They were going to be a real band!

Pretty soon, they were all gathered together in the basement and decided that they would call themselves "The Basement Band," because they were going to practice in the basement. While Jack's parents were down to listen to some of the music *The Basement*

Band practiced, they said that they really liked the band name too.

The rest of the night was a lot of fun. They played popular songs they each knew and introduced each other to new songs some of them hadn't heard of.

The next day, after lunch, The Basement Band members gathered outside for a meeting. The other kids were super excited as Jack came up to them. He saw that the other guitarist, Garrett, was holding a neon green paper with "Talent Show" in big, bold letters.

"Hi!" Jack said, looking at the paper. "What is that?"

Julia, the keyboardist, smiled and said, "It's a school talent show. We can play!" All the other kids had big smiles on their faces and looked very excited.

Jack didn't know how to react. He tended to think about things a little while to see if he liked an idea or not, but he guessed because the rest of his members looked so happy that he should, at the very least, match their enthusiasm, so he smiled. "Wow!" was all he could say as the rest of the band started making plans for performing in two weeks.

At the end of recess, the band decided to meet at least three times a week to be ready for a performance in two weeks. Jack said that he had to get permission from his mom to play in the basement that often, but would tell them all about it tomorrow at school.

At the end of the two weeks, the day of the talent show arrived. *The Basement Band* had practiced a lot and had played in front of Jack's parents two times. They both loved the songs.

But now, as he looked into the crowd from the side of the stage, he realized that it may have been a bad idea. Jack was feeling very, very nervous. The butterflies in his stomach weren't just flapping, they were fluttering, flickering, and flopping all around. He tried to remember what his parents said about being nervous and took a deep breath, but it didn't help. He started to think that the band was going to have to go on without him.

Still, when Jack formed the band, he hadn't thought about actually performing in front of a large group of people, except maybe his family. But his family was still not as big as the crowd of students who were at school to see the talent show.

Jack turned on his heel with his guitar in his hand and almost ran into his dad.

"Hi!" His dad said. "I was just coming back here to wish you luck."

"Oh," Jack said, looking down at his shoes. "I don't think luck will make anything better, Dad. I think that I just need to let the rest of the band go on stage. I don't think I can do it."

Jack's dad kneeled and put his hand on Jack's shoulder, which he gave a little squeeze. "You can do it. You're going to be amazing. I'm sure that it is really hard to remember when you have all the nerves going on inside of you, but you know what you are doing. And, you are really good at it."

Jack looked at his dad. "But I don't feel like I know what I am doing, Dad."

"Exactly. That is what happens when we get nervous. It's hard to remember what

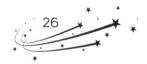

we do and don't know. But, I'm positive that the moment you get out on stage and hit that first chord, everything is going to come flooding back to you. You're going to remember how much you love music, remember how much fun you have with the band, and forget about all the people watching you. You are a very talented and determined kid. I know that you won't let yourself down."

Jack nodded. He was glad his dad understood. "My bandmates don't seem to be worried or nervous, though."

Jack's dad nodded. "Everyone shows their feelings in a different way. You cannot compare yourself to others. You know, it's normal to be nervous. But, even though you are nervous about something, it doesn't mean that you shouldn't do it. Nerves are just your body's way of letting you know how much you care about something, in a good way." Jack's dad patted Jack on the back. "You keep feeling nervous but still do the show. Watch, it's going to be great."

Jack listened to what his dad said and thought about how much sense it made. Jack nodded. He didn't not have to play in the band just because he was nervous. Maybe his nerves would help him play better. Jack knew his dad was right. "Thanks, Dad!" he said. "That makes sense, and I feel better."

When Jack and his band performed, the entire audience jumped up, started dancing, and The Basement Band won the talent show. Jack beamed. He was so happy that he got past his nerves and played with the band. It was one of the best experiences of his life.

~ ~ ~

Don't ever let fear, anxiety, and insecurity about trying new things stop you from making choices. Any time you do something new, you are going to feel nervous. And the more you care about something, the more anxious you will be. Don't let your nervousness stop you from doing anything. You'll miss out on some great experiences.

Connor Presents His Science Project

Do you ever worry about talking in front of people? Do you feel shy? You must know how smart you are. What you have to say is amazing, and people definitely

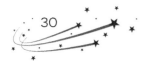

want to hear it, but sometimes shyness can make you not want to say things.

But don't worry! Shyness is just like other feelings, and it doesn't mean you shouldn't do something. It just means that you are afraid of the attention. However, you deserve the attention because you are brave, smart, and amazing, and once you believe in yourself, you will understand that the attention that comes your way is well deserved.

~ ~ ~

Connor is a very smart boy. He is so smart that he won an award for the science project he created and submitted to the local science museum. He likes talking about it with his friends and family, and winning something made him very excited. The museum will have a dinner for all the award winners, and he also gets to pick his favorite type of pasta to eat, which makes the event even more fantastic.

Since the event was a special dinner, Connor even got a chance to wear dress clothes because it would be a little fancy. He wasn't super excited to wear a tie, but his shoes had a special pocket where he could put coins in to make them a little extra special. Placing the coins in his shoes was a lot of fun, so he didn't mind dressing up quite as much after all.

Connor wrote his presentation out and practiced explaining it many times to his parents. He actually rehearsed it so many times that he had his speech memorized. When the night of the museum dinner came, Connor would make sure to bring the notecards he prepared for the presentation.

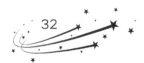

His parents got his science project to set up so he could show how his experiment worked while he presented. Connor looked around the room. He saw that there were a lot of people who loved science, just like he did. He didn't know that so many people would like something so much. And this idea made him very happy and proud to be part of the group that enjoyed science.

At his table, another boy, Alonzo, was sitting there with his family. Connor wanted to ask Alonzo what science project was his, but the food was brought out before he could. Surprisingly, both Alonzo and Connor had rigatoni pasta. They smiled at one another and dug in to eat the food. It was delicious. Connor couldn't imagine anything better than sitting in a science museum with so many people who appreciated learning and being curious about how things worked. He couldn't wait to talk to Alonzo.

After Connor had cleaned his plate, a man came up to the front of the room holding a microphone. He looked very important and official. The man said that each student who won a science award would come up front and talk about their project, why it worked, and how it worked. Then they would sit back down.

Connor wasn't worried about what he would say. But as he looked around the room, he realized that each person there would be listening to what he was going to say. And there were a lot of people.

As the first girl stepped up on stage, Connor started to feel very shy. He turned to look at his mom and dad, who smiled at him. He felt bad about talking

when someone else presented, so instead of telling them about his nerves, he asked his parents to go to the bathroom. They nodded and continued to watch the next student step up to present their project.

As Connor walked through the crowd of people, the room seemed to grow bigger and more full. Now, he was definitely feeling shy. He bit his lip and took a sip of water from the water fountain but didn't go to the bathroom. He tried to come up with a plan where he wouldn't have to talk to all the people, but the idea of not speaking about his science project made him feel very sad.

"Hey, Rigatoni!" Connor heard someone say. Not sure who was named after a pasta, Connor turned back to see Alonzo standing behind him. "That's a lot of people in that room, huh? I'm a little nervous but still happy that I got to come. What do you think?"

Connor looked at Alonzo, who was an older and taller boy. He was surprised that an older student might also feel shy. For some reason, knowing that he wasn't alone in his feeling of shyness helped Connor feel better about the presentation, and he said, "I'm feeling pretty shy, actually."

When he said it out loud, he realized that he felt even better. Getting that thought out of his head and the shy-ness off his chest let him see that there really was no reason to feel so shy. All the people in the room liked science! Plus, they all came to learn about the science projects, right? "Wow," he said. "Just saying it made me feel better. Thank you for sharing your feelings with me too. I'm surprised that you feel worried too. You're older than me! I didn't know older people felt nervous or anything like that."

"Yeah! Everyone always has all the feelings. They don't go away too often, even if you know you have them. My dad says that you have to go through the nerves to get to the good stuff." Alonzo patted Connor on the back. "I think it's almost time for me to show my project. I'm excited to hear what yours is about."

Connor smiled. "Thanks! I'm excited to hear what yours is about too." He had an idea that he and Alonzo would be friends for a very long time.

Connor and Alonzo went back to their table, but Alonzo was called before he could sit back down. Alonzo rubbed his hands together and blew out a big breath. He smiled at Connor and walked past. Connor said, "Good luck!"

"Thanks, Rigatoni!" Alonzo said over his shoulder.

Connor was impressed by Alonzo's presentation and the science experiment he had come up with. He hoped after the special event was over that he would get a chance to talk to Alonzo even more about science. When Alonzo was done speaking, the grown-up presenter brought out a really big trophy for him. A surprise burst through Connor as he had no idea that they were handing out trophies, and he also felt proud that Alonzo had won something. He knew that Alzono deserved it, especially after his presentation.

Connor wondered if anyone else would win a trophy. He snuck a few peeks at

the others who presented already, and it didn't seem that anyone else had one.

Soon after Alonzo walked off the stage, the presenter called Connor's name, and it was his turn to explain his science experiment.

Connor remembered what Alonzo did to calm his nerves down. He rubbed his hands together, closed his eyes, and let out a deep breath before he walked up.

During his presentation, Connor looked around the room as he had practiced with his parents and felt pride when he saw his new friend Alonzo nodding along to his project information. When Connor was done presenting, he showed the group of people how his science proj-ect worked, and when he turned back around to look at them, he saw that they were all standing up and clapping for him.

Connor was handed a wooden plaque with his name on it. It said...

"FIRST PLACE WINNER IN MUSEUM SCIENCE CONTEST."

He was so happy that he held his award to show his parents and saw Alonzo clapping the hardest in the room. It was truly Connor's best night ever.

~ ~ ~

When you overcome shyness, you are showing your bravery. When you intro-duce curiosity into your life, amazing things can happen. When you mix the two, you can have some really good days and nights!

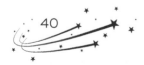

Luke Makes a Movie

Have you ever wondered what you should do when you are bored? It's a great time to get creative! You can make a movie, direct a play, dance around, paint, and

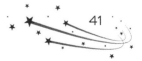

more. The best part about being bored is that you get to use your imagination.

Sometimes, when you use your creativity, things may not come out exactly as planned, but the best thing you can do is keep trying and making your ideas work better because the more you practice or do something, the better you will become!

~ ~ ~

Luke pointed his mom's phone camera at his friends. Inside the screen, they all fit great. They dressed up as his favorite characters from his favorite TV show, and they were getting ready to act out a scene Luke had written by himself. He was very excited and a little nervous.

He had watched many movies and enjoyed writing, but when he got the idea

to make a movie, he was surprised when his mom encouraged him. She even suggested that they use his old Halloween costumes, and she let him use her phone for recording the movie.

When Luke gathered up his friends, they were all excited too. They had been trying to find something to do for the weeks they were off school, and making a video sounded fun and would give them some playtime together. No one realized how hard it would be to write down what the characters in the story would say, but Luke kept everyone going. Any time someone would get down about the project, he would say, "Don't worry! We are going to find another way."

It was because of his never-give-up attitude that Luke's group of friends liked him so much. But today was the first

day of filming, and so far, everything was going really well.

Luke called, "Action!" and his friends started moving in the way that they had planned.

"You, come back here!" the actor said. "You cannot keep the kingdom!"

As the character walked forward, he tripped on a stick, and everyone in the area laughed. Luke laughed with them and called, "Cut!"

They would have to start over again.

Luke realized that making a movie was a lot more difficult than he had ever imagined. There were times before when he would take his mom's phone and film himself having a special "interview" with their cat or the neighbor—he called it

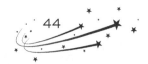

"The Luke Super Show!"—and those times went well, but he didn't have to worry about anyone else other than him, and if he messed up, he would know how to fix it, but with four other people doing the movie with him, things got a lot more messed up than he realized they would.

His friends tripped over things, messed up lines, made each other laugh and dropped items when they shouldn't. Luke saw it all happen. And now, Luke had a lot of mistakes to fix!

Lizzy, Luke's younger sister, wanted to help. Luke asked her to keep the area clean where they were filming the scene. So Lizzy did. She went over to clean up the sticks while Luke went over to instruct his friends. "Okay, guys, let's try to do it one time without any mistakes." They agreed and stepped back into their spots. Lizzy moved back with an armful of sticks, and Luke went to stand next to her. He hit the "record" button again and said, "Action!"

And the characters went through their parts without any issue. Luke was so happy, he couldn't believe they had finally completed their lines without any problems! He was so happy that he didn't realize that he hit the "delete" button on the camera. When he looked down, he went to hit "no" because he didn't want to delete the recording but accidentally hit the wrong button, and the recording deleted itself.

Luke groaned. "Oh no!" he said. He would have to tell his friends about his mistake too. He was a little embarrassed about his error. However, Luke realized that everyone made mistakes and that by sharing his blunder too, they would be

understanding the way he understood when they made mistakes.

When Luke explained that he had accidentally deleted the recording, his friends gathered around Luke and told him it was okay, and they kept going through the video. Luke recorded the first part of the movie without any more problems, but wanted to take a break afterward.

"Making a recording with other people sure is a lot of work," Luke said to his cat, Fidgety, who meowed back at him. "You're right. If I love doing it, it's important to work. Even if I get a little down about the mistakes once in a while. Don't worry, I won't give up, kitty." He scratched his cat's ears and under her chin and then went back to work.

They recorded the other two scenes, and while those had little fumbles and

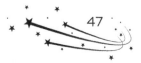

bumbles, whenever Luke became a little flustered by the mistakes, he would take a break, step away, and realize that these things happened, and he didn't want to give up making a movie with his friends.

Luke and his friends spent the next two days together and finished all three scenes. When they were done, Luke gave everyone a high-five and they all hugged together. "Now I have to go and put all the recordings together!" Luke said.

Thankfully, his mom knew how to make videos go together to look like they were a movie, so she and Luke sat down and put the three parts together. They took out the mistakes and any other issues that they could, and when Luke watched the three-minute movie, he realized that it didn't seem like any errors

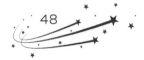

were happening throughout the filming part.

He looked at his mom in wonder. "I can't believe it doesn't seem like there are any issues!" Luke exclaimed. "Wow."

His mom laughed. "Yes, that is why you never give up. You can always find another way, or if you're making a movie, you can edit out the bad parts and just keep the good ones."

"That's great!" Luke said, and he knew now that he wanted his friends to see the video too.

Later that week, Luke set up some chairs for his friends and their parents to watch the movie they had all made together. While it wasn't a long movie, everyone enjoyed it and they ate popcorn. After the movie was over, Luke and his friends came up with a plan to make another one soon.

He agreed that it was a great time and couldn't wait to see what kind of movie they made next!

~ ~ ~

Great moments happen when you keep trying new things, even when there are sometimes mistakes. Never give up! When you don't allow yourself to be discouraged, you can accomplish and achieve amazing things!

Adam is Too Tall

Do you have something different about yourself that you sometimes feel awkward about? Do you know that it is what makes you special? Instead of feeling unsure about it, try to figure how to use

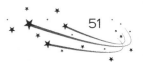

it to your advantage. We are all born with a gift, and it is your differences that make you awesome!

~ ~ ~

As Adam walked to school, he thought about all the new things he would get to learn in a new grade. He was very excited about it and enjoyed school very much. While he had kept busy during the summer, he didn't get to see his friends as much as he used to because he traveled with his family, so he was also looking forward to spending time with them.

When he got to school, Adam walked to his class and passed by last year's teacher. "Woah! Adam, you got tall over the summer, huh?"

Adam nodded and waved but ducked his head a little bit. He had grown quite

a bit over the break. His parents had to buy him new clothes on holiday because of how quickly he grew over the summer. His parents called it a "growth spurt." While his parents explained to him that this was normal and that he was grow-ing into his body, Adam couldn't help noticing how he was almost as tall as his mom. And other people around him treated him a little differently, one lady even called him "sir" at the grocery store and asked him for help reaching an item on a high shelf for her.

Adam was hoping that someone else in his class had had a growth spurt like him, but when he walked into the room, he could see that he was the only stu-dent who was as tall.

Adam's teacher smiled at him as he came in. "Hi, Adam." She pointed to one side of the room. There were small

cubbies where everyone could put their backpacks, coats, and lunch packs. "Go ahead and put your stuff in your cubby, then find your nametag."

After Adam put his lunch box away, he looked around at the desks to find his nametag, which he found quite easily. He was excited because he was sitting in the second row. He liked this because it helped him see the entire board to take notes and listen to the teacher better. When he put his supplies on his desk, he heard someone say, "Mrs. Sullivan?" Adam turned around to look and see that it was a girl who was right behind him. He smiled at her, but she didn't seem to look his way, so he turned around and kept organizing his desk. Then he heard, "I can't see the board with Adam in front of me."

Adam sat upright in his chair, his face began to grow hot, and he was sure he was turning red with embarrassment.

Adam stayed in his chair, and he wanted to keep putting things in his desk, but he was worried about what was going to happen. And before the bell rang to start class, Mrs. Sullivan asked him to move to the back row.

Adam didn't like that at all. He also didn't like the way Lily had embarrassed him in class. He knew that it wasn't his fault that he was taller than some people, but he wasn't sure how to fix it.

At recess, Adam sulked around the play-ground for a little bit. He ignored the kids who asked him to play while he thought about a way to not feel so badly about the fact he was tall. He had grown. His parents said that everyone grew at different rates when they were kids.

As Adam walked onto the basketball court, he nearly missed getting hit by a bouncing ball. When he looked up, some other kids that were near his height and some a little taller asked, "Hey! Can you throw that ball back?"

"Sure," Adam responded. He leaned over to grab the basketball and tossed it back to the group of kids. The tallest one said, "Thanks! You should come play basketball with us."

Adam hesitated, he wasn't feeling great right now, but he realized that walking around feeling sorry for himself wouldn't do him any good, so he decided that playing a game with other kids may be just right for him. He realized that play-ing basketball may help take his mind off the fact that he was so tall, and he went to play with the other kids.

While he was playing the game, it turned out that he also had a great idea for the classroom so he wouldn't be sitting in the back row. He couldn't wait to talk to Mrs. Sullivan after school let out. The rest of the day, Adam was in a much better mood. He had found something he was good at and that he liked. He also realized that he freed up his mind to think of some good ideas by being active.

At the end of recess, Adam thanked the kids, and one of the boys said, "No problem! You should play with us again. You're a great height for playing basketball!" Adam realized that the kid was right and that he did have a good time playing.

Although Adam sat in the back row for the rest of school that day, he no longer felt embarrassed or sad about his place. He understood that it would be important for all other students to see, but his new plan wouldn't have anyone sitting behind any other student. When the bell rang, Adam waited until all the other classmates had left, and it looked as though Mrs. Sullivan was not as busy. He went up to talk to her about his plan.

"Mrs. Sullivan, if we moved the desks in a square shape, all the students would look at each other and still be able to see the board, but no one would have to sit in front of one another. If you'd like, I can help move the desks around to show you how good of an idea it is?"

Mrs. Sullivan smiled. She was very im- pressed by how creative Adam's idea was and wanted to give it a shot. She also said, "I'm sorry that I embarrassed you today in class."

Adam said, "That's okay! If it weren't for the problem, I would have never come up with a new solution. I also might not have realized how much I liked basketball too!"

Mrs. Sullivan smiled again. "Let's move the desks around so no one has to sit in the back of the room, Adam. I'm happy to have you in my class this year. I can't wait to see what else you come up with."

"Thank you, Mrs. Sullivan. Me too!"

The next morning in class, all the other students got very excited. Mrs. Sullivan had to make a new seating assignment, but now no one had to worry about anyone sitting in front of them. While Adam didn't say anything about it, he could tell that the students enjoyed the new shape.

At recess, Adam found the other students who were playing basketball. He jumped right in and played with them and had a good time again. He even got to know some of the other students. They were all the same age, just as tall or even taller than he was, but they were in different classes. So, he was happy he wasn't the tallest kid after all. But he decided, even if he were the tallest, he would have been okay with it.

Coming up with a new idea and finding a new activity he could be part of really helped him feel better about getting tall. He enjoyed the fact that he learned some new things about himself on the first day of school and couldn't wait to find out what else he would know soon!

~ ~ ~

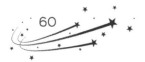

Just because you think you have something different about yourself doesn't mean that you can't turn it into a positive as Adam did. Without the problem he faced, he never would have come up with a better solution. What differences do you have? How can you turn them into something positive? Before you get down on yourself about being different to anyone else, remember how amazing you are. Also, know that any difference you have makes you YOU. Without your differences, you wouldn't be special and unique. No one can do things the way you do them. No one can have your ideas, and no one can be active the way you can be.

If you have a difference you don't understand, see how you can make it your own by joining a club or a team. You can also start to look into new activities

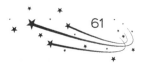

that might interest you. Everyone feels a little weird or awkward sometimes. The point to remember is that no one is those things! Take your difference and turn it into your superpower!

Elijah Builds a Tree Fort

Is there anything that you dream about doing? Did you know that you can do it if you just keep trying? Having a dream and working hard to achieve it is what makes you special and unique. No one else has an imagination quite like you have, and no one can do it the way you can. Remember that even when there are missteps in your journey to reach your goals, you should keep moving forward, no matter what. You can reach your goals and make your dreams come true.

~ ~ ~

Ever since he could remember, Elijah wanted to make a tree fort. His mom said that "tree" was the first word he ever said, and he believed her because he loved being outside. For several years, if Elijah couldn't be outside because of the weather, he would draw pictures of himself outside, and he would always have a tree fort in the picture too.

Although he always wanted a tree fort, his dad said that he had to wait until he was a certain age because of the tools

they would have to use to build it. And now, finally, Elijah was at the right age. Since his birthday was in the colder season, he started by looking for the best outside design for his tree fort. Then he started looking for the best indoor designs for his fort, and finally, he began drawing out his plan to build his perfect hideaway.

Elijah showed his plans to his dad, and then they went to the supply store together to buy all the supplies they would need for Elijah's plans. They got wood, paint, nails, screws, and a few fun accessories that would be added in later.

When they got home, they put everything safely away in the garage so it would be ready for them in the spring. After the wetter part of the spring season passed, Elijah and his dad started working on the floor of the tree fort.

At first, they had to be very careful because they were up in a tree. Elijah's dad had to be in the tree while Elijah had to stand still holding the screws his dad needed to screw the floor together. Eventually, the floor was big enough and stable enough for both of them to stand on it without worrying.

Building the floor of the tree fort took one whole day. And while Elijah was happy it was completed, he never realized it would take that long. They still had four walls and a roof to go. He couldn't imagine how long it would take, but he realized how much work it was.

The floor was the easiest part of the fort, but while Elijah was surprised at how long it took them, he knew that the time and hard work they put into building it would be worth it.

The rest of the tree fort was built on the ground and then lifted into the tree, so Elijah got a chance to help his dad pound nails, use the electric drill, and make different parts of the walls for it. Elijah was pretty impressed with their work when they had finished all four walls but still startled at how much more they had to do. It didn't feel like they would ever finish.

Plus, once they had built the roof and walls, they were heavy. Elijah's dad had to have his friends come over to help them put them up. There were a lot of guys there and their sons. When the dads were putting up the walls, the sons were on the inside using nails to fix it together and help make them stand up straight. There were many moving parts, and Elijah had to be very careful not to hurt himself.

After a long series of setbacks, Elijah was getting ready to give up the idea that the tree fort would ever be ready to play in. But one morning, his dad woke him up and had him look out of the bedroom window. "Look, Elijah! Check it out and see what we did."

Elijah looked out the window and saw the entire tree fort built, just like he had drawn out! "Oh, wow!" was all he could

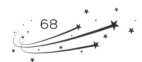

68

say, although his heart was bursting with happiness.

"All you have to do now is to paint the inside and get the furniture moved in there," his dad said.

While he was surprised that there was still more to do, he was too excited that the hardest part seemed to be complete. He was also shocked at how much the fort looked like his drawing. Elijah looked at his dad and gave him a really big, long hug. The hard work they both put in showed Elijah how much his dad loved him, and he knew how special his dad really was.

Elijah couldn't wait to eat that morning. Instead, he ran outside while still in his pajamas, and he even forgot to put shoes on. He climbed up the ladder and opened the door to his tree fort. When he looked around, he wanted to burst, he was so happy. His eyes teared up a little, and he couldn't wait to get in and start painting the walls.

He wanted to make everything be just like he had drawn it, and his dad was helping him do it. Elijah felt like a very special boy to have such a very special dad. He knew right then he had to do something to thank his dad and had a great idea.

The night before Elijah had a big sleepover with friends, he invited his dad up into the tree fort to see how it looked. Now that he had painted every-thing and moved furniture in, Elijah could thank his dad in the way he wanted. So he made him a tree fort surprise dinner!

Elijah's mom helped him prepare it. Even though it was just sandwiches and

popcorn, he knew that his dad would love it. They went to the grocery store to pick out his dad's favorite meats and cheeses and even bought the fancy mustard he liked to put on his sand-wiches. After his dad came home from work that night, Elijah's mom sent him up into the tree fort for the surprise dinner.

His dad was so surprised he said, "I'm really lucky to have such a good son. I love you, Elijah."

"I love you too, Dad. Thank you for all your help with my tree fort."

The next night Elijah had his very first sleepover with his friends who had helped build the tree fort too. His dad didn't stay the night in the fort, but his dad was there for the first part of the fort party. They all drank a glass of juice together and toasted the success of the tree fort.

Elijah and his friends had a great time in the fort that night. They planned on having many more after, too.

~ ~ ~

See? Hard work, dedication, and time spent doing something you love to do pays off in the end. Also, having people there to support you will help you reach your goals no matter how long it takes. Keep going, and you'll get there sooner than you realize!

Make sure to thank everyone who helps you, too. They help you out because you are special, but your love is special for them too. Show them that you appreciate their time, effort, and support, and you will find yourself whole and complete.

Cooper and the Chess Tournament

Do you ever wonder if you are special or if you are strange? What if both words meant the same thing? That you are unique! Not everyone will like the

things you like, and that's okay because you will not enjoy all the things that everyone else likes either. The best thing about who you are is the special and unique things about yourself. And those are the things that no one else can take away from you.

~ ~ ~

Cooper was very excited as he stood in line with his brother and grandfather. He had been waiting weeks for this day to come, and now that it had, he was ready to burst. Today was the day of his very first chess tournament.

A lot of kids that Cooper knew didn't know what chess even was, but he had been playing the game since he could pick up the pieces, and he really, really enjoyed it. He played chess with his brother, his dad, and his grandpa. They

played at least once a week together, and for Cooper, that was normal.

A few weeks ago, just after he had signed up for the tournament, Cooper found a book about chess in his school's library. He was curious about it, so he checked it out. When he was walking into the hallway, a couple of his class-mates stopped him, looked at the book, and asked, "Chess? What is chess?"

Cooper didn't realize that not everyone knew about chess, so he answered in the best way he could. "It's a fun game!" He walked away, eager to read through the book, and didn't realize that the other boys were still trying to talk to him about it.

The next day when Cooper was at lunch, the group of boys came up to him again and said, "Can you explain your game?" Cooper looked up from his book and smiled. He said, "Chess is a really fun game. There are a bunch of squares on the board, and you get to take the other player's pieces. Whoever gives their king the inability to move, wins!"

While the boys looked confused by the explanation, Cooper didn't let that bother him. Instead, he opened the book that he was reading to show the other students some of the pictures. He figured that the photos might explain things better.

"So, you get to make a bunch of different moves to win?" one of the boys asked curiously.

"Yup. I play all the time with my brother, dad, and grandpa. I'm actually joining a tournament in a few weeks. It's where many chess players come together, and

they all play games against each other. Eventually, they knock one player out at a time until one person is left!"

The boys looked interested. "Maybe we could come and watch?"

"Sure," Cooper said. "That would be a great way to learn about chess too."

Throughout the next few weeks, Cooper had taught the group of boys more about chess and had even played games against them. He also practiced with his brother, dad, and grandpa to get all different experience levels against him.

Now, it was time for the tournament to start, and when Cooper looked around, he saw his new friends and his family there rooting him on. One of his new friends from school had even joined in on the tournament, although he was on the beginner level, which meant that he and Cooper wouldn't play each other.

When the tournament started, Cooper shook his opponent's hand, because that was good sportsmanship. They both sat down at their station and listened to the rules. Fifteen games were going, which meant that thirty players were on the same level as Cooper.

That is so many people! Cooper thought.

And it was a lot of people. The chess tournament took a few hours, and each time a new game started, that meant that there was one person who had been knocked out of the tournament. Soon, Cooper looked around, and it was only himself and one other player, a girl who was his age and had red hair. He smiled at her and was surprised that he was one of the last two players! That meant

he was one person away from winning the tournament.

They shook hands and sat down at their spot. Since she was the younger player, she got to move first. As Cooper watched her make her first move, he tried to figure out what her next move would be and where he should put his piece first. The game moved quickly, and it was obvious that she had practiced just as much chess as he had before the tournament.

A few times, Cooper was worried he couldn't get out of the spot she had put him in, but at the last moments, he found a way out, and soon, he had captured her king! He was the winner of the tournament and was so surprised.

He looked up to see all his new friends and his family clapping for him. When he turned to the girl he had just played, she said, "Good game!" and put her hand out for him to shake.

Cooper got a big trophy and had spent a whole day doing something he loved to do. He couldn't wait to join another tournament and to do it all again.

~ ~ ~

When you love something, put all your heart and soul into it. Don't worry what other people think if they don't under-stand your passion. You will inspire others to do what they love and be themselves as well. You are special and unique, and there is only one of you. Embrace who you are, and you will go far!

Julian Learns Something New

When someone is different or looks different than you do, what do you think? Do you believe that they are a nice person? Do you wonder what they are like? Or do you try to stay away from them because you aren't sure about their differences? Learning about new people who are different from you is a good thing. Always remember that asking questions is better than ignoring the differences, and you'll have a chance to learn some really amazing things about the world.

~ ~ ~

Julian has gone to the same school his whole life. He has lived in the same house since he was born, and he has even had the same dog for that same time. Although he knew about new places and new things because his parents took him on vacations, went to museums a lot, and ate a lot of new types of food, Julian had never really experienced anything too out of the ordinary, so when a new girl came to school, he became very excited.

The new girl said to call her Hannah, but that her Korean name was Ha Yoon. The teacher instructed Hannah to sit next to Julian, and he waved and introduced himself. "I'm Julian. It's nice to meet you," he said.

Julian stuck out his hand to shake hers, and she took it. Her lips broke into a big smile, and she shook his hand in a really big way. Julian and Hannah laughed together.

At lunch, Julian motioned for Hannah to sit next to him and some of his other friends, which she seemed grateful for.

"Thank you," she said. "I didn't know if I would make friends on the first day of school or not."

"Where are you from?" Julian asked. She spoke English very well, but it was clear that it was not her first language.

"I just moved from Seoul, Korea."

At that moment, another group of students came over and sat down at the next table. They were very loud, and Julian had difficulty listening to what Hannah said because she spoke so softly. Instead of continuing, she gave a quick nod, and they both began opening their lunch boxes. Julian pulled out his normal sandwich, fruit, and a snack, whereas he saw Hannah pull out a bowl of something red.

His curiosity piqued again.

Hannah took the lid off of the bowl, and a big smell drifted out of the container.

"Oh my! What is that smell?" A girl from the loud group of students yelled. "It smells so gross!" She held her nose and looked over at Hannah. The girl pointed

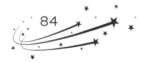

at Hannah and said, "Oh, boy! It's her! She smells!"

Hannah's cheeks started to blush and she began to look ashamed.

Julian sniffed the food, and while it didn't smell familiar, he didn't think it smelled that bad. Julian stood up and said, "It is NOT Hannah. It's her food. I think it smells good. You should sit down. Unless you have something nice to say to her or you want to ask her about her lunch, we don't want to hear anything you have to say."

Julian sat back down and turned to Hannah, who had a big smile on her face now.

"Thank you," she said and held out the bowl for him to see. "This is kimchi. It is vegetables in a red sauce. You can try some if you'd like."

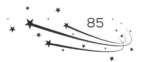

85

And he did. It was a new taste he hadn't tried before, and he really liked it too, but Hannah explained that it was home-made from Korea and he was excited because he had never had food that came from a whole other country be-fore. "That's exciting!"

After lunch, the loud kids came over and started talking to Hannah too. They apologized for being loud, and the girl even asked Hannah about her kimchi, what it was made of, and how it tasted. Hannah taught all the kids some Korean words and said that she would make sure not to bring kimchi to school every day because it did smell so strongly, but that she would bring other food that her mom would make for her and that they could all try some.

When the other kids left, Hannah hugged Julian. "Thank you for being so

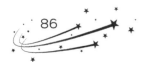

kind today. I didn't realize that things would be so different here. But they are. Would you teach me more about how you and your family live? I will teach you more about Korea and my family too. Maybe you could even come over and play sometime?"

Julian was excited to learn more about Korean culture and was excited to go to Hannah's house. He said, "Sure!" right away. "Let me talk to my mom as soon as I get home."

He was also proud of the louder students who came over afterward to apologize for their behavior. Julian was also surprised at himself for standing up for Hannah. It wasn't hard to do, and it seemed like he helped her make a lot of new friends too. Overall he thought his day went pretty well.

When he went home that night, he told his parents about kimchi and asked if they could make some together.

His parents told him that they were proud of the job he did today, and they even gave him an extra helping of dessert for being such a good friend. Julian couldn't wait to go back to school and learn more about Hannah, her food, and Korea.

~ ~ ~

When you look at all people as different and know that you can learn something from everyone, you never have to be afraid of how they look, talk, dress, or act, especially if it is not the same as you. Everyone has something wonderful to offer, especially if it is something you've never experienced before.

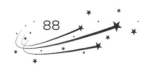

Dylan and the Tree Swing

Have you ever dreamt of doing something exciting? Do you think about what it would be like soaring through the air? Do you think about flying like a bird or swimming like a fish? If you dream about doing daring things but worry about the outcome, don't fret! Trying

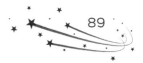

new things can be a bit scary, but you aren't alone with your fears. Remember, safety always comes first, but next comes adventure!

~ ~ ~

Dylan lived in a great neighborhood. There were kids of every age living in almost every house on his block, and they were all really good friends. Any time a new kid would move into a house, the group of children would run up to them, say, "Hi!" and ask them to play right away. This way, none of the kids on the street ever had to feel left out.

Near their neighborhood was a lake they could all swim in when the weather was warm, and they would spend hours down at the water together. If they

weren't swimming, they were fishing. If they weren't fishing, they were building a boat. If they weren't building a boat, they were playing in the sand. There was a lot of stuff they did, and they all did it together.

The one thing they couldn't do together was jump off of the tree swing into the water. The parents had decided that they weren't allowed to jump from the swing until each child was a certain age. All the parents on the street agreed with this rule, and every kid followed it. The parents explained that jumping off a tree swing when you were too young could have some serious safety issues, so when Dylan became old enough to jump off the swing, he was thrilled.

Dylan jumped out of bed that morning and realized how he was finally old enough to jump into the water off the swing. He had been watching his friends jump off the swing for years. And now it was his turn!

He rushed around to get dressed. He made his bed haphazardly and raced to grab his swim trunks and towel. His mom and dad slowed him down. "Woah! You have to eat breakfast first, and then you have to wait for the rest of your friends to wake up and get ready. You cannot go down to the lake by yourself."

Dylan scrunched up his nose. He knew that was also a rule he had to follow, but he danced around on his toes because he was so excited. He didn't know when anyone else would be awake, so he turned to his dad and said, "If I eat breakfast, will you come with me?"

His dad laughed and said, "You have to eat breakfast anyway. But, yes, after you eat breakfast and your food settles, I will go down to the lake with you."

Dylan ate his breakfast as slowly as he could. But he chewed a lot quicker than normal. By the time he was done, and his dad had gotten ready to go down to the lake, he knew his breakfast had settled.

As they walked down to the lake, Dylan felt that they were walking too slow and he wanted to move faster! When he tried to walk quicker, his dad explained to him that everything seemed to be moving slower than normal because of how eager he was to try something new.

His dad said, "Try to stay a little bit calmer and enjoy this time right before your new adventure."

Dylan thought it made sense, so he took a few deep breaths, which seemed to calm his anticipation. When they got to the tree swing, Dylan and his dad set

down their stuff, and then suddenly, Dylan realized how high the tree swing was from the ground, and then he noticed how far away it was from the water.

He had seen lots of kids jump from this swing, but it had never seemed to look like this before! Dylan turned to his dad. "Why does the swing seem so much bigger than I've ever seen it?"

His dad placed a hand on his shoulder and knelt next to Dylan. "Because this is your biggest adventure yet. Trust me, once you get on the swing, you'll realize that it is the same size and the same distance away as it has always been. If you'd like, I'll push you to get you going and let you know when it's a good time to jump."

Dylan nodded, he was really happy his dad was here, and when he went to sit

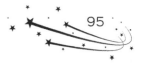

95

on the swing, he saw that the lake didn't seem quite so far as it originally looked, but his stomach got tangled in his excitement, and a smile burst out across his face, he was finally going to jump!

As his dad pushed the bottom of the swing, Dylan heard a loud noise from over his shoulder. He turned his head to the left and saw all his neighborhood friends watching him and cheering him on. He swung once, twice, three times. "Jump now, Dylan!" he heard his dad call.

Dylan let go of the ropes and launched himself forward into the air. For a few seconds, he could feel the wind in his hair and the breeze on his face. When he saw the water coming close, he pulled his knees up into his stomach, held his breath, and landed like a cannonball with a GREAT BIG SPLASH!

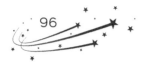

When Dylan popped up from the water, he threw his fist in the air. His dad was right. The rest of the people at the shoreline were jumping and clapping for him. He was so excited. He couldn't wait to have fun with all his friends and to do it again and have fun all together.

He ran out of the water, wet and proud of himself, and his dad scooped him up into a big hug. Now Dylan was ready for his next adventure.

~ ~ ~

Never be afraid to dream too big or dream too much. Anything is possible when you play safely, follow the rules, and head for your best adventure. You are going to surprise yourself with how much you can do, and never let fear stop you!

Sebastian and His Brother Build a Rocket

Is there a person in your life you look up to? Do they teach you new things and listen to your stories? Do they help you

out with problems and inspire you to be creative? If so, you are very lucky! These people are called role models, and they are here to help you out, especially when the times are tough. Think about how you would say thank you to your role models for always supporting, loving, and guiding you toward the right answer.

~ ~ ~

Sebastian and Mark are brothers but are very different in age. Mark can drive, he goes out with his friends and works part time at a grocery store. Sebastian just wants to play with his trucks and chase his friends around the playground. Even though they are so different in age, they are very close friends. Mark takes time out of his day every day, to come and see Sebastian. He always asks his younger brother what he did, how he ate, and about school.

Sebastian would tell him, but then also ask Mark about his day too. After homework, dinner, chores, and part-time work were finished, Sebastian was usually in bed. But there would be days when Mark would come into his Sebastian's room just to read him a story—Although his parents pretended that it was a secret, they did know about the stories and thought it was a nice thing for an older brother to do.

Because Mark was getting so busy with school and part-time work, he wanted to make sure that he still spent time with Sebastian, so he suggested that they spend a few hours together every weekend. Sebastian thought that it was a great idea and a nice way to be together.

For their first ever "guys" day hang out, Sebastian asked their parents if they

could help him buy a rocket kit for him and Mark to put together. His parents were happy that Sebastian was interested in building something, and they said, "Yes, we would be happy to."

The Friday before they went to hang out together, Sebastian and his mom went to the store to look for rocket kits. They had quite a few in the toy section, and since he was serious about wanting to find the best kit available, Sebastian took his time to find the one that he felt was just right.

He read the instructions on the boxes, looked at the pictures, and didn't pick the one that cost the most money or the one that had a battery-operated super-blast engine—although he did want to pick that one up later. He picked out a rocket that looked easy to build and something they could put together in the park. The rocket was powered by water and used recycled material!

Sebastian thought this was great because Mark always talked about treating the planet well.

He couldn't wait to surprise Mark with the rocket and then see it take off together. The next morning, Sebastian poked his head into his brother's room and said, "Hey! Wake up! I have a surprise for you!"

Mark rolled over and said, "What is that?"

"It's a rocket kit! We get to make it together today. All we need is a bicycle pump. Plus, we can make it at the park."

"That sounds great, little brother. We'll have to get all our homework and chores done for the day before we can go."

Sebastian nodded and rushed out to eat breakfast.

After breakfast, he did his homework and tidied up his room. He also took the trash out for Mark so he wouldn't have to. When he was done, Mark was getting his coat on and said, "Alright, little brother, let's go!"

Sebastian and Mark drove to the park with the rocket kit and the bicycle air pump in the back seat.

When they got there, they found a picnic table to sit down at so they could lay out all of their supplies and read the instructions. They went through each item they were supposed to have and made sure that everything matched the instructions. When they were done checking everything out, Mark put his hands on his hips and said, "This is a really cool rocket kit. Great pick! It's awesome that the supplies come from recycled material and that the rocket is powered by water."

Sebastian beamed. He knew it was the right rocket to pick, but hearing Mark say he liked it made him feel really good too.

Mark and Sebastian worked together as a team. One would read out the instructions, and the other would hand over the supply that was needed. It didn't take long at all and after about fifteen minutes, the rocket was ready to launch.

Mark went to fill the bottle up with water, and Sebastian got the bicycle pump ready. In the next few moments, Mark had pumped the rocket up with air, and Sebastian was just waiting for the final signal to let the rocket go. When Mark

yelled, "Go!" Sebastian removed his hand from the bottle and with a loud *Wooosh!* the rocket took off. Sebastian got even more excited. As he watched the rocket soared through the air, he started jumping around in amazement and excitement.

Sebastian surprised himself that they could build something so simple yet so very cool. He would never forget this day as long as he lived.

They got to shoot off the rocket a few more times and even started to draw a crowd of people who were interested in what they were doing. "Hey! What is that?" someone yelled.

"It's a rocket we built from a rocket kit," Mark said. "My awesome brother picked it out."

Sebastian didn't think that the day could get much better.

After a few hours, they did have to leave the park because Mark had to go to work, and on the way home, Sebastian fell asleep. He dreamt of rockets and rides, and space, and stars. He dreamed of going on all the adventures with his brother, and he was happy.

When he got home, Mark left for work, and Sebastian got to tell his parents all about their day. He was definitely curious about other rockets and would start doing more research about them after dinner. He realized that not only did he have a great day with Mark, but he also developed a new interest in something too.

After he ate, he started looking up more about model rockets and tried to find

the best kit for the next time they would go. Soon after, Sebastian was ready for bed, and Mark came home from work.

This time, Mark brought home a story about space, and when he read it to his younger brother, Sebastian drifted off into a good sleep and had more rocket dreams.

~ ~ ~

What do you think? What would be your special way to spend time with your favorite person? How would you like to thank them and let them know how much they mean to you? Do you want to tell them with words or show them with action? You could make them something or create something for them, and when they see it, they'll know how very lucky they are to have you in their life.

Epilogue

Now that our stories are done, do you have your own to tell? Did you see the boys and their amazing stories? Do you see their great adventures? Do you know how special you are, unique boy? Your interests, ideas, creativity, and thoughts are what make you amazing. Whenever you feel afraid or nervous to do something you dream about, take a deep breath and do it anyway. Challenge your fear and nerves and remember how you are going to accomplish great things in the world.

When you are ready to tackle a new journey, jump in with your feet first, and shine your special light as bright as you can for as long as you can.

You are smart. You are funny. You are interesting. You are amazing!

Bonuses
Our Gifts For You

Subscribe to our Newsletter and receive these free materials

Scan Me

www.specialartbooks.com/free-materials/

Stay Connected with Us

Instagram: @specialart_coloring
Facebook Group: Special Art – Kids Entertainment
Website: www.specialartbooks.com

Impressum

For questions, feedback, and suggestions:

support@specialartbooks.com

Nadia Ross, Special Art

Copyright © 2021

www.specialartbooks.com

Images by © Shutterstock

Made in the USA
Middletown, DE
28 July 2023

35893900R00064